TORNADOES, HURRICANES, AND TSUNAMIS

A PRACTICAL SURVIVAL GUIDE

April Isaacs

The Rosen Publishing Group, Inc., New York

Published in 2006 by The Rosen Publishing Group, Inc.
29 East 21st Street, New York, NY 10010

First Edition

Library of Congress Cataloging-in-Publication Data

Isaacs, April.
Tornadoes, hurricanes, and tsunamis: a practical survival guide/
April Isaacs.—1st ed.
    p. cm. —(The library of emergency preparedness)
Includes bibliographical references and index.
ISBN 1-4042-0533-0 (lib. bdg.)
1. Emergency management—Juvenile literature. 2. Natural disasters—
Juvenile literature. I. Title. II. Series.
HV551.2.I73 2006
363.34'923—dc22

                                              2005017630

Manufactured in Malaysia

On the cover: *Left:* A tornado hit Turner County, South Dakota, in June 2003. *Middle:* A NASA satellite image shows Hurricane Rita spiraling over the Gulf of Mexico in September 2005. *Right:* Tidal waves washed two boats ashore in Sri Lanka after a tsunami hit Southeast Asia on December 26, 2004.

CONTENTS

Introduction

Around one o'clock in the morning on December 26, 2004, a major earthquake hit near the coast of Sumatra, Indonesia, in the Indian Ocean. The earthquake registered 9.15 on the Richter scale, an earthquake of gigantic proportions and the second largest yet recorded. The earthquake was so huge that aftershocks were reported in parts of the western United States. However, it was not the earthquake but the tsunami that was produced by this earthquake that caused billions of dollars worth of destruction to virtually every coast along the Indian Ocean. A tsunami is a circular pattern of waves that moves shoreward from the source of its disturbance (in this case, the earthquake). The 2004 Indian Ocean tsunami spread a large distance, as far as 5,300 miles (8,530 kilometers), stretching all the way to the shores of Sri Lanka, India, Thailand, and even eastern Africa.

Meanwhile, beachgoers and residents went about their daily business, completely unprepared for the danger that was upon them. Because tsunamis rarely occur in the Indian Ocean, there was little cause for residents to panic when waters receded and the ground mildly shook. Many people later claimed they thought these indications were caused by the tides going out or a minor earthquake that had occurred somewhere deep under the ocean.

Floodwater from a tsunami swirls through a village in Sri Lanka on December 26, 2004. The region was not prepared because there was no tsunami warning system in place.

However, when the tsunami finally hit, it claimed more than 300,000 lives (the exact number of deaths might never be known). Even though the tsunami took hours to reach land, most people were unaware of the impending danger and were caught completely off guard. Why had there been no warning?

The major failure contributing to the lack of preparedness for the 2004 Sumatra tsunami was that there was no tsunami warning system set up in the Indian Ocean. A tsunami warning system is a network of sensitive oceanic sensors that can detect when a tsunami is developing. These sensors allow government officials and scientists to warn communities in time to dispatch orders for people to evacuate to higher ground before the disaster strikes. Having a tsunami warning system, such as the one in Japan, has greatly reduced the number of casualties and injuries that have resulted from a tsunami. However, because countries near the Indian Ocean had little experience with tsunamis, people had a false sense of security thinking that they would not have to be prepared for tsunamis.

Although it came at a high price, there was a major lesson learned from the Indian Ocean tsunami: being prepared for disaster at all times can save people's lives. In the following chapters of this book, you will find information about how to prepare for tornadoes, hurricanes, and tsunamis, whom to call for help, ways you can reduce damage to your home, and even tactics that can save someone's life or your own.

1 What Is a Tornado and What Do You Do If One Hits?

Perhaps you've seen tornadoes that have been filmed for movies or TV. They're typically depicted as gigantic funnels that scurry along the ground, picking up everything from cars to farmhouses inside their large, swirling cyclone. But did you know that tornadoes are not always large moving funnels? Sometimes the only way to identify one is to spy airborne, spinning debris that seems to move in the same direction from one wind force.

Tornadoes are powerful windstorms that occur during an existing thunderstorm or hurricane. During this storm, a change in wind speed and direction can begin to produce a funnel. When cold air passes over warm air, the warm air rises and causes the winds to gather momentum in a swirling cone shape. Tornadoes pack an incredible amount of wind force. A tornado can grow as tall as 50,000 feet (15,240 meters) and have wind speeds reaching upward of 300 miles per hour (480 kilometers per hour). That's 50 percent faster than the top wind speed of most category-five hurricanes (the most powerful type of hurricane, which can have wind speeds of 156 miles per hour [251 km/h]). Tornadoes have the power to hurl automobiles and even small houses and mobile homes more than 100 yards (90 m) from where they once stood. They are most destructive when touching ground, typically no longer than twenty

Two violent tornadoes rotate around each other near Dimmitt, Texas, in June 1995. The tornadoes were so forceful that they ripped up highway pavement and caused more than $12 million in damages.

minutes. However, tornadoes can touch ground numerous times and can change their direction and backtrack in a matter of seconds. Because tornadoes form very rapidly, are extremely powerful, are not always visible, and have unpredictable patterns of movement, they are among the most dangerous and life-threatening natural disasters. There is little time to predict the formation or approach of a tornado, so weather services do not have much time to issue warnings to the public or instructions to take shelter. The National Oceanic and Atmospheric Administration (NOAA), which monitors the entire United States for storms and tornadoes, can warn of an oncoming tornado only about twelve minutes before it happens. That doesn't allow much time to take shelter, so the best way to avoid damage to your home or yourself is to prepare for the disaster beforehand.

Tornado Basics

Most tornadoes occur between the hours of noon and midnight, so these are the times of day and night to be on a heightened alert. Tornadoes usually occur from March to August. From March to May is the peak season for southern states, while northern states see the most tornado activity from late spring to early summer. Though it is unlikely, tornadoes can occur at any other time during the year. During tornado season, your school or local community center may initiate an awareness day or week during which you can find out more information about emergency preparedness for tornadoes. If no such programs exist, talk to your school principal or local officials and encourage them to start an awareness program.

The United States is hit by more tornadoes each year than any other country. On average, there are approximately 1,000 tornadoes reported every year. Tornadoes can occur anywhere in the United States, but most often they form in the Midwest, Southeast, and Southwest. Tornadoes have been reported in mountains and in valleys, in deserts and in swamps, from the Gulf Coast to Canada, in Hawaii, and even in Alaska. Tornado intensities based on wind damages are classified on the Fujita scale with ratings between 0 and 5. An F0 storm is the weakest and an F5 storm is the strongest. Two percent of these highly violent tornadoes—F4 and F5—can cause a path of destruction more than 1 mile (1.6 km) wide and 50 miles (80 km) long.

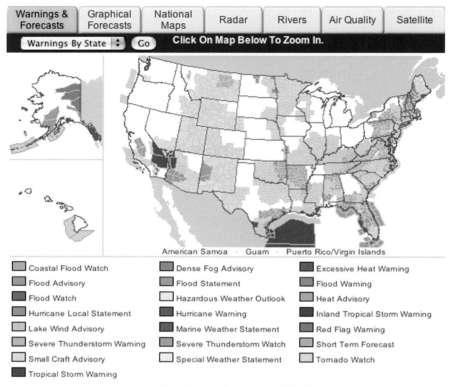

| Warnings & Forecasts | Graphical Forecasts | National Maps | Radar | Rivers | Air Quality | Satellite |

Warnings By State ⬍   Go   Click On Map Below To Zoom In.

American Samoa · Guam · Puerto Rico/Virgin Islands

- Coastal Flood Watch
- Flood Advisory
- Flood Watch
- Hurricane Local Statement
- Lake Wind Advisory
- Severe Thunderstorm Warning
- Small Craft Advisory
- Tropical Storm Warning
- Dense Fog Advisory
- Flood Statement
- Hazardous Weather Outlook
- Hurricane Warning
- Marine Weather Statement
- Severe Thunderstorm Watch
- Special Weather Statement
- Excessive Heat Warning
- Flood Warning
- Heat Advisory
- Inland Tropical Storm Warning
- Red Flag Warning
- Short Term Forecast
- Tornado Watch

Last update: 07.19.05 - Tue - 05:14:12 PM (EDT)

The National Weather Service, an agency within the National Oceanic and Atmospheric Administration that provides the public with timely weather forecasts and warnings, displayed this map of Hurricane Emily on its Web site (http://www.nws.noaa.gov) in July 2005. A tornado watch was issued for part of Texas.

They are responsible for nearly 70 percent of all tornado-related deaths. Scientists still don't know everything there is to know about tornadoes or how to predict an approaching tornado sooner than twelve minutes before it strikes. Experts can only guess, based on past tornadoes, which weather conditions are more likely to produce a tornado. Consequently, coming up with a plan and practicing tornado drills is your best defense against this natural disaster.

Preparing for the Worst

It's important to know what to do before a tornado hits. Having a tornado survival kit, a ready shelter, and a family plan can ease panic and save lives. Knowing how to contact your local emergency management office or Red Cross chapter, knowing how to identify warning signals, and designating a safe place to take shelter are your best defense against tornadoes. Also, it's a good idea to keep a record of your belongings in case they are damaged during a tornado—photographs and/or videotapes of valuables and your home's interior and exterior are usually required when making insurance claims after a disaster. These photos and videos, along with other important documents,

Tornado Drills

If you live in a tornado-prone region, you might already be familiar with tornado drills. Many schools will have regular tornado drills that teach students the sound of a tornado alarm, how to exit the classroom single-file, and how to sit to avoid being hurt by broken glass or other flying objects. Schools usually predetermine which areas in the school building are safest, such as a windowless interior hallway on the ground floor. The best way to sit during a tornado drill is with your knees tucked in to your chest and your head down and facing a wall. Fold your hands around your neck to further protect yourself from flying objects. If your school does not have regular tornado drills, talk to your teacher or principal about starting them.

Eighth-grade students in South Carolina practice a tornado drill at a middle school. To protect yourself during a tornado at school, tuck your knees to your chest and keep your head down while facing a wall and covering your head with your hands (or a textbook, like these students have done).

such as birth certificates, credit cards, social security cards, bank statements, and health and home insurance information, should be kept in a fireproof and waterproof safe.

Before a tornado hits, sit down with your family and locate an appropriate room or area for shelter, called a wind-safe room, which has been reinforced. This shelter should be away from any windows. Basements make ideal shelters. If you do not have a basement, stay in a window-less room, such as a bathroom or closet, on the ground floor. Try to avoid doors and outside walls. The center of a room is safer than the corners because objects tend to be drawn to corners if wind forces move them. You might want to get underneath a sturdy desk for additional protection from flying debris or broken glass.

If you live in an apartment building, take shelter in the building's basement, the lobby on the lowest floor possible, or an interior room with no windows. Do not use elevators during a tornado. Take the stairs instead. To be better prepared for emergencies, get to know the floor plans and building exits ahead of time.

If you live in a mobile home, find a safe building nearby where you can take shelter. Mobile homes are easily swept up by high-speed winds and are unsafe places during a tornado. However, you can take preventive measures to

A tornado in Alabama hurled this mobile home through the air in May 2004. If mobile homes are not secured to the ground, they can easily be swept up by high-speed winds. Although tie-downs for mobile homes are always good to have, they still may not save the home from being tossed through the air during a tornado or hurricane. It's best to seek shelter elsewhere.

lessen damage to your mobile home should a tornado strike. Tie-downs extending from the base of the house to secure heavy stakes in the ground can prevent your home from being uprooted during a storm. These should be professionally installed and inspected every year. Although tie-downs can save your mobile home from destruction, they do not make it a safe place to stay during a tornado. Even if you have tie-downs installed, it is important that you still evacuate your mobile home and get to a safe shelter during a tornado.

If you live in a house, talk to your parents about building a shelter in your home. The Federal Emergency Management Agency (FEMA) has information on plans for designing and building a tornado shelter. (See the For More Information section at the back of this book.)

You should also make a disaster survival kit beforehand and keep it in or near your shelter so you won't have to waste valuable time gathering up supplies or looking for the kit during an emergency. This kit should include items that can be used for most emergency situations, including tornadoes, hurricanes, and tsunamis (see pages 15 and 16). Determine whether your kit will be used in a home-based shelter or for evacuations, and pack it accordingly. This kit should be checked every year to make sure the contents are fresh and in working order. Keep the survival kit in an easily accessible place, either in the trunk of the car in which you will evacuate, in your hall closet or garage, or in the predetermined shelter space in your home. Planning ahead and putting this kit together before a disaster strikes can save you valuable time that you may need for other preparedness steps.

DISASTER SUPPLIES KIT

✓ **First-aid kit** You can purchase a first-aid kit from your local drug store. It should include various sizes of sterile bandages and gauze pads, antibiotic ointment, alcohol wipes, aspirin, hypoallergenic tape, safety pins, scissors, tweezers, a blanket, hand sanitizer, disposable gloves, a cold pack, and ipecac, a syrup used in treating accidental poisoning (use only if recommended by the poison control center).

✓ **Prescription drugs** Be sure to bring any essential medication that is prescribed to you, a family member, or a pet.

✓ **Flashlight and extra batteries**

✓ **Battery-operated radio with extra batteries or wind-up radio**

✓ **Nonperishable foods** It is best to supply food that needs no refrigeration, cooking, or water. These might include canned meat, vegetables, and juices; or prepackaged food such as peanut butter and granola bars. If you put canned food in your kit, remember to include a nonelectric can opener. Obtain the foods that may be needed by elderly people, infants, or people who have special diets.

✓ **Water** You should make sure that you have 1 gallon (3.8 liters) per person per day, and at least a three-day supply. The drinking water should be stored in a nonbreakable, sterile container. You will only need to drink approximately 64 ounces (189.3 centiliters) of water per day. The rest of the gallon would be used for bathing and mixed with dried foodstuffs such as powdered milk or soup.

✓ **Food, water, and supplies for your pet** These may include newspapers, a litter box, water and food dishes, and toys.

✓ **Cash and credit cards (and bank account numbers)**

(continued on following page)

(continued from previous page)

✓ **Essential documents** These include insurance papers; identification cards; birth, death, and marriage certificates; social security cards; the deed to the house; car title; a list of all your possessions in your home; medical records; wills; and tax documents. Keep these documents in a waterproof and fireproof container.

✓ **Appropriate, comfortable clothing** Bring a warm sweatshirt or jacket and comfortable shoes (no open-toe shoes). Include some work gloves in case you need to pick up broken glass or other sharp objects.

✓ **Rain gear** This includes waterproof boots, a slicker or poncho, and a hat.

✓ **A small tool-kit** This kit should include basic tools such as screwdrivers, screws, a hammer and nails, a wrench, and pliers.

✓ **Sleeping bags or blankets**

✓ **Toiletries** These items should include toothpaste, toothbrushes, liquid soap, deodorant, and antiseptic wipes. If you are traveling with or caring for a baby, pack the appropriate hygienic items, including diapers.

✓ **A spare set of keys for your home and vehicle**

✓ **Extra gasoline** Ask an adult to put this away in a safe place.

✓ **A cell phone and a charger for it that will work in the car** In case there is no power, you can recharge your cell phone using the car's battery.

✓ **A whistle to use when calling for assistance**

✓ **Paper products** This includes toilet paper, tissues, paper towels, and feminine products.

✓ **Plastic bags of various sizes to be used for waste disposal**

You and your parents will need to designate an emergency contact. This contact can be a family friend or a relative. Members of your family should have this contact person's phone number and address on hand at all times in case you are separated from one another. Make sure that all your family members, especially your younger siblings, know how to dial 911 or your community's emergency number and ask for the appropriate assistance.

Conduct periodic tornado drills so that everyone remembers what to do. Prepare your house by keeping trees and bushes trimmed. Remove items that may become flying missiles in the tornado winds. Install permanent shutters that

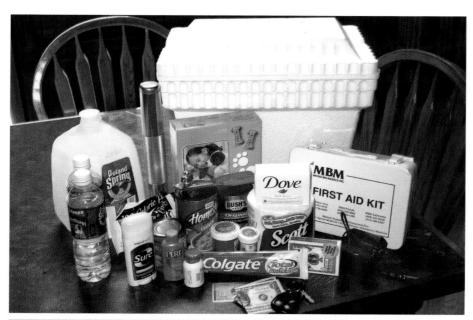

A disaster supplies kit should be available in every household. Make sure your kit includes water, a flashlight, canned food, and a manual can opener. Your kit should be kept in a container and in a place where it is easy to grab during an emergency. Ensure that everyone in the house is familiar with the kit's location.

can close over windows and strengthen garage doors. This will block wind from applying pressure to walls inside the house and lifting off the roof.

What to Do When a Tornado Strikes

Learn about your community's warning system, because different communities have various ways of providing warnings. Some have sirens that are intended for outdoor purposes. All make NOAA weather radio announcements. Make sure you know the name of the county or parish where you live because tornado watches and warnings are issued by county or parish names.

If the right weather conditions occur, such as increased wind speeds and heavy thunderstorms, your local weather service may issue a tornado watch. When a watch is issued, double-check to make sure that all your family members remember where to take shelter. Keep the radio or television tuned to local channels or the NOAA radio announcements (the primary alerting system of the National Weather Service [NWS]) in case there are additional announcements or instructions for your community. The NWS encourages people to buy a weather radio that is equipped with the Specific Area Message Encoder (SAME) feature that will alert you to tornadoes in your area. Stay away from cafeterias, supermarkets, shopping malls, or other places where the roofs have to span wide spaces.

There are a few ways to know if a tornado is about to touch down. The sky is typically a greenish color. Sometimes, you may hear a loud sirenlike whistle or a roaring noise that is like the sound of a freight train. This is the sound of high-speed winds shaping into a funnel and developing force. Before a tornado hits, the sky may seem calm and eerily still. Also, if you spot swirling debris in the air, this could be a sign of a developing tornado.

When your local weather service issues a tornado warning, it means that an actual tornado has been spotted. Because tornadoes are unpredictable and can change direction at any moment within a matter of seconds, you should take shelter immediately, no matter where the tornado appears to be heading. You MUST make the decision to take shelter before the tornado arrives. It may be the most important decision you will ever make. During a

This Oklahoma City, Oklahoma, resident builds a storm shelter into his garage floor in 2003. Oklahoma is often hit by tornadoes, and in recent years, families have prepared for natural disasters by building storm shelters in or near their homes.

An employee of the Federal Emergency Management Agency (FEMA) stands next to a safe room in Stockton, Missouri, in 2003. The safe room is made out of steel and is reinforced with wood. FEMA provides information to the public about how to build a safe room for the home.

tornado warning, go to your shelter (with your survival kit) and keep the radio turned on for further updates. If you have pets, elect a member of your family to be responsible for collecting each pet.

But what if you are not at home or at school during a tornado? What do you do if you are outside? However minor a storm may seem, it still has the potential to grow into a violent, powerful, and life-threatening situation. If you are in a car, listen to the radio. Most radio stations will issue weather and traffic updates every hour, if not more frequently, during a storm. Ask the driver to take you to the nearest building and take shelter until the storm subsides. If you aren't near any building where you can take shelter, get out of the car and lie flat in a ditch or on low ground. Avoid overpasses, bridges, road signs, and power lines. Place your hands over your neck and pull your knees to your chest. Remember that the lower to the ground you are, the more susceptible you are to flooding from the thunderstorms that preceded the tornado. It is important to be cautious of even the smallest amount of

A tree landed on a house in Port Clinton, Ohio, in November 2002, after a tornado hit the area. Never leave a shelter during an emergency situation unless authorities have said it is all clear. Once a tornado touches down, even if briefly, it can leave and return to the ground and even backtrack.

standing water because it can be a drowning hazard or it can sweep you off your feet. Never, under any circumstances, try to outdrive or outrun tornadoes because they move very quickly and randomly.

The Aftermath of a Tornado

Even if it appears to be safe to leave your shelter, you must not do so until you have been given instructions from your local authorities or weather service. As discussed earlier, tornadoes are unpredictable and can backtrack in seconds. So if you think a tornado has passed and that you are out of danger, remember to always be on guard.

After the weather service or local emergency authorities have announced that it is safe to leave your shelter, enter your home with caution. Because tornadoes have such powerful winds, hazardous materials such as bleach, gasoline, or other chemicals may have shifted and spilled during the storm. If you see any spilled items or broken glass, avoid the wreckage and immediately tell an adult. If power or telephone lines have snapped or loosened during the storm, avoid them and report the dangerous conditions to your local telephone or power company.

If you have taken shelter outside during a tornado, wait for clear skies before getting up from your protective position. A good sign that a tornado has passed is the clear skies that usually follow directly behind it. Beware of perilous debris on the ground that can cut or trap you.

Tornadoes can be quite violent and sometimes can uproot tall trees and other objects that could fall on people and trap them. If someone is trapped or injured, do not attempt to move him or her. Any additional movement could possibly worsen that person's condition. Call 911 or your local emergency number immediately and wait for assistance.

If your home has been damaged by an especially violent tornado, have your parents contact their insurance company to see what repair costs will be covered. If the insurance does not cover the damage or if you are uninsured, FEMA and the American Red Cross can offer tornado victims some financial and legal assistance, and temporary housing in certain cases. Make sure that you and your family photograph the damage both inside and outside of the building for the insurance claims.

2 --- Hurricanes and Hurricane Preparedness

A hurricane is a severe tropical cyclone that affects coastal areas, usually near or around tropical and subtropical regions where the water is warm. Hurricanes are powerful thunderstorms with high-speed winds of more than 74 miles per hour (118 km/h) that circulate in a counterclockwise direction (in the Northern Hemisphere). These winds and rainstorms circulate around a calm center known as an eye. In the eye of a storm, conditions may seem like they're improving, but they can possibly get worse. Hurricanes originate near or on the equator and spread heat from the equator to the Northern Hemisphere. Hurricanes also bring rain to drier lands that would suffer drought without them. Although hurricanes are vital, they can be very destructive to the areas in their paths.

The hurricane season lasts in most areas from early June until late November. More than twenty tropical storms (depending on the region and weather conditions) can be produced during these months. Most hurricanes occur during the peak part of the season, between August and September. Hurricanes have ripped through areas spanning several hundred miles, causing floods, wreckage, and death. If you live in an area that is prone to hurricanes, it is essential to be prepared for them. Knowing what to do

This NASA satellite image shows Hurricane Wilma spiraling in the eastern Gulf of Mexico and Tropical Storm Alpha in the western Caribbean Sea on October 23, 2005. Weather officials estimated Hurricane Wilma's winds at 125 miles per hour (200 km/h) when it hit Florida, near the city of Naples. At the time it made landfall, Hurricane Wilma was classified as a category 3 hurricane, and as the eye of the hurricane moved across the state, a powerful storm surge caused massive flooding in the Keys.

before a hurricane arrives, during a hurricane and possible evacuation, and afterward could save your life.

How Much Damage Can a Hurricane Cause?

The damage caused by a hurricane can be immense. Hurricanes produce violent winds that can uproot buildings and trees and toss cars around as if they were pebbles. Each year there is an average of ten tropical storms worldwide; about six of these become hurricanes. They tend to develop over the Atlantic Ocean, Caribbean Sea, and the Gulf of Mexico. Many of them remain over the ocean and never hit land. On average, five hurricanes strike the United

States' coastline every three years, with an average of two being a major hurricane of category 3 or higher. The most powerful hurricanes to hit the United States, such as Hurricane Camille (1969) and Hurricane Allen (1980), had recorded wind speeds of 190 miles per hour (305.8 km/h). Sometimes the heavy winds displace large amounts of water from the ocean to land, as Hurricane Katrina (2005) did in New Orleans. This is called storm surge, and it causes serious and sometimes deadly flooding. Hurricane winds can produce tornadoes that are also very destructive. These tornadoes can pick up and throw around heavy objects, which can come crashing down on you or your home. However, the most dangerous aspect of a hurricane is the inland flooding it causes, which is responsible for most of the deaths that occur from hurricanes. Inland flooding happens when the rainfall from a hurricane floods an area that can be as much as 100 miles (161 km) away from the storm. Inland flooding often causes millions of dollars worth of damage and death. In 2005, Hurricane Katrina flooded most of the Gulf Coast, and thousands of people died from the floods. Even if you don't live near a coast, you still need to be aware of approaching hurricanes and be prepared for potential inland flooding.

The first thing to do to prepare yourself for a hurricane is to find out whether your community is at risk of experiencing hurricanes. Hurricanes develop in seven major places, which are referred to as basins. These basins are found near the coasts of China, Japan, Australia, Africa, and India. There are two basins that affect areas of North America: the North Pacific Ocean, which affects California, western Mexico, and

Hawaii; and the North Atlantic Basin, which affects Central America, the Caribbean, eastern Mexico, and most of the eastern coastal areas of the United States. A hurricane from the North Atlantic Basin can travel up the eastern seaboard and reach as far north as Canada. If you live near any of these areas, check with the Tropical Prediction Center that cooperates with local, state, and federal agencies for updates through the NWS. These hurricane-monitoring centers track hurricanes and issue storm watches and

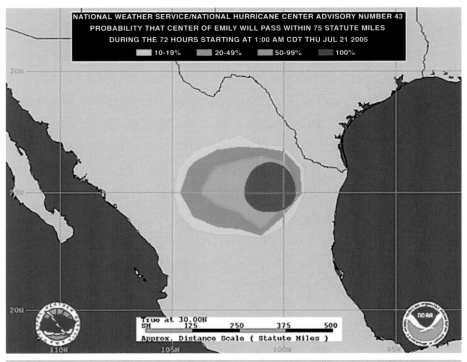

On the Web site of the National Hurricane Center (http://www.nhc.noaa.gov) of the National Oceanic and Atmospheric Administration (NOAA), this map showed Tropical Depression Emily in July 2005. Each percentage given in the caption describes the probability of the center of the tropical cyclone approaching the corresponding location on the map.

warnings. If you live in or near California, Hawaii, or Mexico, get updates from the Central Pacific Hurricane Center, which is located in Honolulu, Hawaii (http://www. prh. noaa.gov/hnl/cphc). If you live near the Gulf of Mexico, the Caribbean, or the Atlantic Ocean, check for hurricane updates from the National Hurricane Center, which is located in Miami, Florida (http://www.nhc.noaa.gov).

Identifying the Storm

Both the National Hurricane Center and the Central Pacific Hurricane Center are part of the NWS. They forecast and monitor tropical weather activity from the mildest tropical storms to the most violent and gigantic hurricanes. Typically, both centers can forecast an approaching storm thirty-six hours before it hits land and can issue a warning. The NWS will issue a hurricane watch if conditions are conducive to hurricanes. When a hurricane watch is issued, it means that there is a threat of hurricane or tropical storm conditions within thirty-six hours and you should leave the radio or television on to keep up to date as the storm develops. If a hurricane warning is issued, you should begin preparing yourself for the oncoming storm that is expected within twenty-four hours or less and be ready to evacuate if directed to do so by local authorities.

The greatest threat from a hurricane is the storm surge. It is a mountain of water that can be 20 feet (6 m) high at its peak and 50 to 100 miles (80 to 161 km) long.

The Saffir-Simpson scale is used to rate a hurricane's intensity, and wind speed is the deciding factor in the scale. There are five classifications of hurricane intensity

Rubble fell from buildings in downtown New Orleans, Louisiana, after Hurricane Katrina, a category 4 hurricane, battered the Louisiana coast on August 29, 2005. A category 4 hurricane can cause severe and extensive damage, as Katrina did to the coastal regions of Louisiana, Mississippi, and Alabama. Hurricane Katrina became the most destructive and costliest natural disaster in U.S. history,

for Atlantic hurricanes, called categories. A category 1 hurricane is the mildest hurricane and has a wind speed of 74 to 95 miles per hour (119 to 153 km/h). During a category 1 hurricane, there can be some coastal flooding, plants may get uprooted and small boats or unanchored mobile homes may be overturned, but little, if any, damage is done to buildings. A category 2 hurricane, with winds from 96 to 110 miles per hour (154 to 177 km/h), will cause major damage to mobile homes, cause some damage to roofs, piers, doors, and windows; and uproot trees and shrubs. In some cases, people who live near the shore are asked to evacuate for their safety. A category 3 hurricane, with winds from 111 to 130 miles per hour (178 to 209 km/h) will blow over trees, damage buildings, and cause serious flooding along the shore and perhaps inland, and mobile homes can be destroyed. A category 4 hurricane, with winds 131 to 155 miles per hour (210 to 250 km/h) will cause widespread damage and most often will require the evacuation of people living 500 yards (457 m) from the shore and those living in one-story housing or homes with unstable foundations, such as mobile homes. A category 5 hurricane is the strongest and most destructive, with winds of more than 156 miles per hour (251 km/h). It has the power to overturn buildings, blow out windows, and rip telephone poles and streetlights from the ground. These hurricanes also cause major flooding to the ground-level floors of all buildings along the shore. The conditions during a category 5 hurricane are usually so intense and dangerous that it is imperative to evacuate to within 5 to 10 miles (8 to 16 km) of the shore. Remember that the calm eye of the storm is deceptive and is not the end of the storm. Once an eye passes over an area, the winds increase and come from the opposite direction. Many people have been surprised and injured by the second opposing wind by venturing out too soon after the first wind in the storm passed.

Evacuation

Depending on the strength of a hurricane (that is, its category classification), the NWS may advise you to leave the affected area. If you are advised to evacuate, you must do so immediately, or you will find yourself in the midst of some life-threatening conditions, such as floods, powerful winds, and storm surges.

The American Red Cross chapter that is located nearest you will provide you and your family with up-to-date evacuation routes. It is important that you follow these routes and not your own, as roads may be flooded, damaged, or blocked and could delay and even prevent your exit. Always keep your local American Red Cross branch's phone number handy and in a place where your family members can find it.

In the event that you have to evacuate, make hotel reservations before leaving your home. If you cannot reserve a hotel room, the American Red Cross will direct you to community shelters that have been set up for hurricane refugees.

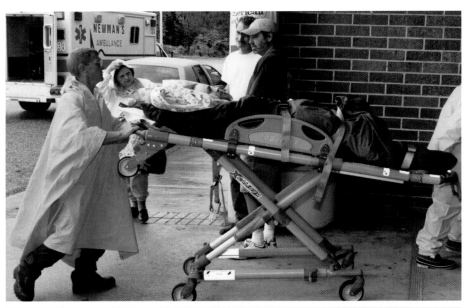

During Hurricane Ivan in September 2004, emergency medical technicians evacuate a person with special needs and take her to an American Red Cross shelter in Mobile, Alabama. The American Red Cross provides the public with information about evacuation routes and shelters. Make sure you have the contact information for your local Red Cross chapter.

Before leaving your home, it is important to have a parent or guardian turn off the gas, water, and electricity to avoid home damage or unsafe conditions upon your return.

But what do you do if a hurricane hits while you are at school and your parents are at work? Road blocks, flooding, and bad conditions may make it difficult for your parents to get to you. This is why it is vital to have an out-of-state emergency contact before a hurricane threatens and you are separated from your family. An out-of-state contact may be a relative or a family friend who can relay information between you and your family during such an emergency. During hurricanes and other disasters, local calls are typically difficult to make because phone lines are busy. Before evacuating, it is important to call your out-of-state emergency contact to let him or her know exactly where you are going and when you are leaving. If you get stuck on the road or in dangerous conditions during evacuation, this information can be passed on to an emergency rescue team, who will able to locate you more easily. Figure out whom your family should have as an emergency contact and make sure that all family members know his or her phone number and address.

In case you may one day have to evacuate because of a hurricane, your parents or guardian should always make sure that your family vehicle is in proper working condition. They should also keep some extra gasoline (stored in the appropriate fuel container) in a safe place. Road blockage and traffic may extend your evacuation for more than an hour and you do not want to get stranded if your vehicle runs out of gas. Furthermore, if there is a power outage, gas stations may not be able to pump and distribute gasoline from their tanks.

This hotel in New Orleans, Louisiana, allowed guests to bring pets during Hurricane Ivan. Most American Red Cross shelters do not allow pets. Before a hurricane hits your area, determine which shelters and hotels will allow you to bring pets during a disaster. You can also check with a veterinarian for boarding facilities.

If you have pets and you will need to evacuate to a shelter, call the shelter beforehand to find out about its pet policy. Many emergency or disaster shelters will not accept pets, so you will need to make arrangements with a hotel, motel, relative, or friend beforehand for your pet's safekeeping. You may be able to arrange emergency boarding for your pets through the American Society for the Prevention of Cruelty to Animals (ASPCA). If your local ASPCA does not offer boarding, it will provide you with information about other boarding options. You may also want to check with your veterinarian about kennels or humane society shelters that will be safe for your pets during emergencies. Remember to make sure that your pet is wearing an identification tag and that the pet's vaccinations are current.

What to Do If You Are Not Evacuating

If a hurricane is mild enough or if you live far enough away from coastal areas, you may not be advised to evacuate your home. However, if you are not evacuating, this does not mean that you aren't at risk during a hurricane. Even a category 1 hurricane can cause flooding and damage. According to information posted on FEMA's Web site (http://www.fema.gov), a person can be swept away by only 6 inches (18 centimeters) of water. Even the mildest hurricane can be dangerous, as winds can climb to more than 74 miles per hour (119 km/h). Because of these

This homeowner in Wrightsville Beach, North Carolina, attached shutters to his house in preparation for Hurricane Isabel in September 2003. To protect your family's home during a hurricane or severe storm, obtain window shutters made of thick wood or shatter-resistant plastic. Check with local authorities for what the building code stipulates for minimum protection against natural disasters.

strong winds, flooding, and potential storm surges, you must take shelter. If you are at school during a hurricane, your teacher or principal will know where to take you. If you are at home, the best place to take shelter is away from any freestanding heavy objects, such as bookcases or clocks, and away from windows. If the power goes out, turn off all appliances in your home to prevent a surge when the power comes back on.

There are also ways to protect your house from hurricane damage and make it a safer shelter in the storm. Talk to your parents about strengthening the exterior of your home, especially reinforcing the anchoring of the roof. In some hurricane-prone regions, there are already building codes that require homes to have a certain level of security against hurricanes. However, in most cases, these safety measures are only the bare minimum and cannot fully protect your house against damage. Fitting the windows with thick wooden shutters that you can lock and seal during a hurricane can greatly reduce the chance of harmful broken glass flying into your home. Storm shutters can be made of basic plywood, which offers the minimum protection, or polycarbonates (thick, durable, shatter-resistant plastics), which offer the maximum protection to your home. Check with your local building codes to find out how thick the plywood should be for your windows (some areas of Florida, for example, recommend a thickness of at least 7/16 inch [1.12 cm]). You should attach the plywood to the exterior of the windows using double-headed nails. The types of materials your home is made of will determine what kind of anchor to use. For example, if your home has heavy masonry, you will want to use thick masonry screws to attach the plywood shutters. Make sure that the holes for screws have been drilled and the anchors installed before the hurricane season, and that the shutters have been precut and labeled as to which cover goes with which opening so that you can board up the house quickly. Some organizations, such as the Federal Alliance for Safe Homes (see the For More Information section at the back of this book), recommend materials and products that have been tested and certified to withstand hurricane-strength winds.

Making a Hurricane Survival Kit

Whether you are evacuating or taking shelter in your home, there are several items you will need to keep together in a safe place for emergency use during a hurricane. (See chapter 1 for information about what to include in your survival kit.)

Make sure to keep this survival kit in an easily accessible place, preferably in the predetermined shelter space in your home. Planning ahead and putting this kit together before a hurricane disaster strikes can save you valuable time that you may need for other preparedness steps.

When Is It Safe to Leave the Shelter and Return Home?

After a hurricane has passed, make sure you keep the radio on to listen for instructions from the local authorities. When you definitely know that the hurricane has passed and the proper officials have given the all-clear signal, check to make sure that your family members are together and are safe. Use the following checklist when first returning home:

- Search for broken power lines, but keep away from them. These should be immediately reported to your local power company. Do not step in any water if there is a possibility of "hot" electrical lines being down; you could be electrocuted.

- Inspect the house's foundation and exterior to make certain that the house is safe to enter. Take photographs of all the damage.

- Be on the lookout for snakes or potentially dangerous animals that may have been washed into your home during floods. If you do find wild animals near or inside your home, avoid them and immediately notify your local ASPCA.

- Open the windows and doors. During the hurricane, there may have been flooding, and your home could have water damage. Opening windows and doors will help air out your home.

- Use your phone only for emergencies. After a hurricane, local lines are usually busy. Unnecessary phone calls can prevent others from reaching emergency centers for getting help with serious problems.

If your home has been badly damaged from the hurricane, your parents' or guardian's insurance policy may offer some assistance. If your family does not have insurance to

In July 2005, FEMA's mobile Disaster Recovery Center helped people apply for aid after Hurricane Dennis damaged areas of southern Alabama. FEMA offers various services regarding property damage for hurricane victims.

cover the damage done to the home, FEMA offers a number of services to hurricane victims, including financial assistance, arrangements for temporary housing, and legal help. Have one of your parents or a guardian call FEMA (for contact information, see the For More Information section). If you have lost touch with a family member or friend, the American Red Cross keeps a database of lost people. In the database, they can file someone as missing or check to see if that person has left any contact information. In the event that your family's emergency out-of-state contact is unreachable, make sure all family members know to call the local chapter of the American Red Cross as a backup plan.

3 ... Tsunamis and Their Aftermath

Contrary to popular belief, a tsunami is not a stronger type of hurricane. A tsunami is caused by an underwater earthquake or volcanic eruption. This disturbance sends a series of waves riding to the shores. However, not every underwater earthquake will create a tsunami. Usually, tsunamis are produced from earthquakes involving convergent continental plates (one plate moves on top of another and pushes the weaker plate beneath it). When these plates shift, they cause some of the most violent and powerful earthquakes and, consequently, some of the most devastating tsunamis, such as the 2004 Sumatra tsunami, which claimed the lives of more than 300,000 people.

From the disturbance's point of origin, waves can reach speeds of more than 450 miles per hour (724 km/h). Tsunamis are not like typical waves that circulate water at the surface. Instead, tsunamis circulate water to the depths of the ocean, which means that they carry a gigantic amount of force and can travel long distances, sometimes more than 1,000 miles (1,609 km). As tsunami waves come within miles of the shoreline, the waves shorten and decrease in speed. For coast guards and boaters, it may appear as though the waves are no threat to the land at all. In fact, the word "tsunami" is a Japanese word for "harbor wave," which boaters who were far from shore thought them to be. When you are far out on the

At a United Nations World Conference on Disaster Reduction in Kobe, Japan, an engineer explains how digiquartz broadband depth sensors (called tsunameters) work. Created by Eddie N. Bernard, the director of the NOAA's Pacific Marine Environmental Laboratory in Seattle, Washington, the tsunameters were being used as part of the Pacific tsunami early warning system in 2005. They measure small changes in pressure on the seabed and transmit the information acoustically to the surface buoy, and then via satellite to the warning center.

ocean, a tsunami can appear to be a tidal wave that poses little threat to the shore. However, moments before reaching the shore, tsunami waves slow down and can burst into walls of water more than 100 feet (30 m) high and come crashing mercilessly down on the beach. The tsunami can displace millions of gallons of water, causing some of the worst devastation of any natural disaster.

Where Are Tsunamis Likely to Hit?

Tsunamis affect coastal areas, in particular, surfaces that are below or just above sea level. Residents or vacationers on or near beaches or coasts are the most at risk of experiencing tsunami waves. The higher the elevation of the surrounding area, the better your chances are for not seeing a tsunami.

Tsunamis are most common in Japan, although they can occur in any coastal place where earthquake or volcanic activity can agitate the water and generate enormous

≋USGS

Northern Sumatra Earthquake of 28 March 2005

This seismic hazard map from the U.S. Geological Survey in July 2005 shows the March 2005 earthquake near northern Sumatra, Indonesia, and the December 2004 earthquake and aftershocks. The National Earthquake Information Center (NEIC) issues bulletins such as this to help the public prepare for the likelihood of the occurrence of earthquakes and tsunamis. The Pacific Ocean, for example, is vulnerable to tsunamis because of the great number of earthquakes that occur there.

waves. The Pacific Ocean is most susceptible to tsunamis because of the high number of earthquakes and the volcanic activity that occur there. Nevertheless, although it is rare, the Atlantic Ocean is also at risk for having tsunamis. The United States has a few major areas that have shown seismic activity and that are more likely than other areas to produce tsunamis. The northwestern Pacific coast, which includes the states of Washington, Oregon, and California, are at the greatest risk because of the fault lines along the Cascade Mountains. Experts predict that in the event of a northwestern Pacific tsunami, residents and tourists would have little warning to evacuate before the tsunami hit. Other states at a greater risk for tsunamis are Hawaii and Alaska. Remember this rule: the larger the earthquake, the greater potential there is for a tsunami. As soon as you hear news about an earthquake, even if it strikes far away from where you live, be prepared to evacuate to higher ground—generally, 100 feet (30 m) above sea level—or to an inland area, about 1 mile (1.6 km) or farther inland, if possible. You can learn more about earthquake and volcanic activity by consulting the National Earthquake Information Network (http://www.eqnet.org), which frequently posts information about seismic activity that is happening around the world.

What to Do Before a Tsunami Hits

One of the biggest reasons that a tsunami can be so devastating is that there is little warning when one is approaching. Sit down with your family and discuss the following ways to prepare for a tsunami. Whether you live

A tsunami buoy is pictured here aboard the NOAA ship *Ronald H. Brown* in the Pacific Ocean in April 1998. Had a buoy such as this one been used in the Indian Ocean in 2004, seismologists and other scientists might have been able to forewarn people in Indonesia and elsewhere that there was the threat of a devastating tsunami after the December earthquakes.

in an area that is at risk for tsunamis or you are vacationing in a state or country that is at risk, it is important to discuss these issues:

- If you live in a coastal community and feel a strong earthquake, you may have only a few minutes until a tsunami arrives, so DO NOT wait for an official warning. Quickly move away from the water and to higher ground. If you notice a rapid rise or fall of coastal waters, it may be an indication of a tsunami.

- Know the evacuation routes. Do not trust your own route of evacuation. Roads may be blocked or you may experience heavy traffic. Your community's American Red Cross branch will be able to give you up-to-date information about the safest and quickest exit roads to travel to higher ground.

- Make sure your parents know that they need to have a reliable vehicle in case of an emergency. Keeping spare gallons of gasoline in a safe place is a good practice.

- Keep abreast of all earthquake, volcanic, and landslide activity that is occurring near your residence or vacation spot.

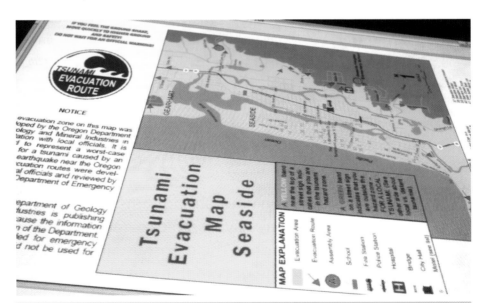

A nonprofit partnership called RAINS established an alert program, the Connect and Protect Program, and distributes NOAA and NWS bulletins and evacuation plans from a base in Alaska to all businesses, schools, motels, restaurants, hospitals, and other organizations in the Pacific Northwest. The image pictured here is a tsunami evacuation map for Seaside, Oregon.

- Find out whether your home or vacation spot has a tsunami warning system. You can contact the local weather dispatcher or government official for more specific information about the threat of tsunamis in that area. The tsunami warning center for the United States is called the Pacific Tsunami Warning Center and is located in Hawaii.

- Make a disaster survival kit. Keep this kit in a safe and practical place where you can quickly grab it, such as in your family's vehicle. (See chapter 1 for more information about what items to include in a disaster survival kit.)

- Designate an emergency contact. If you are vacationing in a tsunami-prone area, make sure your emergency contact knows your hotel information, what your plans are during your stay, and how to reach you if there is an emergency.

- If you hear about a tsunami watch, it means that a tsunami has not yet been verified, but could exist and may be within an hour away.

- If you hear about a tsunami warning, it means that a dangerous tsunami may have been generated and could be close to your area. The report usually includes the arrival times and the geographic area that may be affected by the tsunami.

Things Not to Do When a Tsunami Strikes

What shouldn't you do during a tsunami? Try to follow these helpful guidelines:

- Don't panic. Panic only worsens your situation. Panicking during a tsunami can cost you valuable time and even your life.

- Never watch the waves come in. Because a tsunami wave can be mesmerizing, most people are tempted to stand and watch it come in, thinking they will have enough time to run or drive away from it. Nonetheless, if you can see a tsunami wave, it is already too close for you to escape it.

- Do not return to the beach or your home unless you have been told that it is safe to do so by local authorities. One of the biggest and deadliest mistakes that people make during a tsunami is assuming that tsunamis are just one gigantic, crashing wave. In fact, tsunamis produce multiple waves that can arrive moments to hours after one another. Listen to the radio constantly during a tsunami to find out from experts and helicopter teams when the tsunami has actually finished its course.

After a Tsunami

You will only know when a tsunami is over when it is reported by your local authorities. A tsunami's magnitude cannot be predicted by the average layperson. Seismologists, weather service personnel, and coast guard officials are highly trained in knowing the nature and behavior of tsunamis and will inform you when it is safe to return to lower lands and beaches.

If it is safe to return to your home, make sure you carefully inspect the premises with the help of an adult. A tsunami's

Residents clean up debris from their community in southern India on December 30, 2004. Massive tsunamis smashed the coastlines of India, southern Asia, and eastern Africa after the earthquake that seismologists measured as 9.15 on the Richter scale off Indonesia's coast four days earlier. Cleaning up after such widespread devastation can take months or even years.

force can cause damage to houses and power and telephone lines, so if you find any broken or loose power lines or telephone lines, report them immediately to your phone service or power company using a cell phone or a neighbor's phone. Do not step in any water that might have an electrical wire in it because you could be electrocuted. Look for fire hazards, gas leaks, and damage to sewer and water lines.

Beware of heavy flooding generated by the tsunami. Flooding can cause home damage, wash unwanted and sometimes dangerous ocean-dwelling creatures into your home, and generally threaten your safety. Even if there is only a small amount of water, do not underestimate its dangers. It does not take very much water at all for a person to drown, and only 2 feet (61 cm) of water can carry a car away. Your parents should avoid driving after a tsunami, but if they must drive, they should do so only in the case of an emergency.

With the help of an adult, check around your neighborhood for any trapped or injured people. Do not move any injured person. Wait for professional emergency assistance. Many people may need cardiopulmonary resuscitation (CPR) due to the heavy flooding of the tsunami. If you are unfamiliar with first-aid and CPR methods, you may want to take a course to learn about them at the American Red Cross. You might be able to save someone's life someday.

If your home is safe to enter, open the windows and doors to allow the air to dry it out. Shovel out any mud that may have seeped inside. Clearing out debris, mud, and dirt will shorten the drying process. Once the walls are dry, use bleach or a heavy disinfectant to clean the walls.

If your family's home has been destroyed or badly damaged, have your parents call your insurance company right away. You may want to take pictures of the wreckage for the insurance claim. The insurance company, depending on your family's plan, may be able to cover the cost of repairs. If you are uninsured or your insurance policy does not cover these costs, you can get in touch with FEMA or American Red Cross agencies, which offer a variety of assistance programs for victims of natural disasters.

Emergency Preparedness and Your Community

Natural disasters are not preventable, and in some cases they are necessary for the earth's geological cycles. There is no way to stop a tornado, hurricane, or tsunami from hitting your residence or community. Emergency preparedness is key to lessening the damage, injury, and even death that can occur during natural disasters such as these. Knowing as much as possible about the storm's typical characteristics, keeping informed by listening to or watching the local weather service programs on the radio or television, knowing exactly how to get to safety, and making a disaster kit can help prepare you for any of these disasters.

Once you've prepared yourself and your family, getting active in your community about disaster preparedness and relief services can be beneficial to you and the community and may save several lives. Ways that you can increase storm awareness in your community include the following:

- Contact your local American Red Cross office and find out about the community programs for emergency preparedness. The American Red Cross offers free classes in several types of first aid and CPR procedures. Encourage all of your friends and family members to take these courses.

A young volunteer *(top)* from Lakeland, Florida, hands out pet food at a donation site in nearby Wauchula in August 2004. Hurricane Charley wreaked havoc on Wauchula, and volunteers like him raised money to buy food and supplies and handed them out. In January 2005, Prince William and Prince Harry *(bottom)* of Great Britain packed supplies for the victims of the Indonesia tsunami during a Red Cross relief effort in Bristol, England. Volunteering can bring much-needed relief to people during natural disasters.

- Find out whether your local newspaper or news station posts any regular information about storm emergency preparedness. If they do not, encourage them to do so. Most deaths from natural disasters occur because people are unaware of how to act during an emergency.

In 2005, the *St. Petersburg Times* printed a special report on how to be safe at home during hurricane season; the online version of the report is shown above. The newspaper included articles about protecting homes during hurricanes, stocking a disaster emergency kit, safeguarding important documents, making evacuation plans, keeping pets safe, and learning about what communities can do to prepare for hurricanes during the off-season.

- Volunteer. The best way to increase emergency preparedness is to find out how you can help improve awareness. Passing out brochures, lending a hand at a demonstration, donating blood to disaster victims, or offering clerical services can be major contributions. Contact the American Red Cross, FEMA, your local office of emergency services, or NOAA (see the For More Information section for contact information) to find out how you can help.

- Living through a natural disaster such as a tornado, hurricane, or tsunami can be an emotionally devastating experience. If you or others you know have lost a

In January 2005, fourth-graders in Johnson City, Tennessee, collected pennies for the tsunami relief effort in Southeast Asia. Fund-raising for relief services is one way to help people who have been affected by a disaster.

loved one or been significantly affected by a tornado, hurricane, or tsunami, contact your school guidance counselor or teachers about getting help. They can direct you to find people who have been trained to assist those in need.

- Start a fund-raiser. You can come up with all sorts of ways to raise money for relief organizations. Hold a bake sale, and ask your friends, family, and teachers to contribute baked goods for the cause. Another way to fund-raise is to organize a walk. This activity is something you will probably need to do in conjunction with your community center because paths and roads may need to be blocked for your walkathon.

Helping out in your community before or during a disaster can save lives. If everyone learns to be prepared, the devastation caused by tornadoes, hurricanes, and tsunamis will be less catastrophic. Most natural disaster deaths and injuries are the result of ignorance of what to do in emergency situations. So, become educated about these natural disasters and practice preparedness techniques before the next tornado, hurricane, or tsunami strikes!

Glossary

category A class of hurricanes; category 1 hurricanes are the mildest and the category 5 hurricanes are the most powerful.

CPR (cardiopulmonary resuscitation) A method used to restore normal breathing to a person who has gone into cardiac arrest; it includes clearing air passages to the lungs, giving mouth-to-mouth respiration, and massaging the heart by exerting pressure on the person's chest.

drill A rehearsal for how to act and where to go during an emergency.

emergency contact A predetermined relative or family friend who can act as a point of contact for you and your family members during an emergency.

emergency preparedness A state of being aware of and ready for disasters.

evacuation Leaving an area (such as your home or vacation spot) that has been declared unsafe by local authorities.

evacuation route A course of travel from endangered areas to safe areas that has been mapped out by local authorities.

first aid Emergency medical treatment that is given to injured persons before professional medical assistance can be obtained.

first-aid kit A collection of medical supplies that includes bandages, aspirin, antibiotic cream, and other medical materials.

flooding An overflowing of water onto land that is normally dry.

hurricane A severe tropical cyclone, originating in equatorial regions with surface winds of at least 74 miles per hour (118km/h).

hurricane warning A notice that sustained winds associated with a hurricane are expected in a specified coastal area within twenty-four hours. Hurricane warnings are usually followed by emergency instructions.

hurricane watch An announcement to specific coastal areas that a hurricane is within thirty-six hours.

inland flooding Floodwater produced by a hurricane or other storm that reaches areas as far as 100 miles (161 km) away.

National Oceanic and Atmospheric Administration (NOAA) A division within the U.S. Department of Commerce that predicts environmental change and provides scientific information to governmental officials and the American public.

National Weather Service (NWS) A government agency within the National Oceanic and Atmospheric Administration that employs a variety of scientists and uses satellite technology to forecast weather conditions for the purpose of issuing regular weather reports to the public.

Specific Area Message Encoder (SAME) A system used by the National Weather Service to encode the

Emergency Alert System in the United States for radio, television, and cable broadcasts.

storm surge A rise above the normal water level along a shore caused by strong onshore winds.

survival kit A pack of necessary supplies that have been gathered together and stored in a handy container before a disaster strikes, for use during an emergency.

tornado A violent cyclone of high-speed winds, which occur during thunderstorms or hurricanes.

tornado warning A statement issued by the National Weather Service indicating where a tornado has been spotted. Tornado warnings are usually followed by emergency instructions.

tornado watch A statement issued by the National Weather Service when weather conditions are favorable for the occurrence of tornadoes. A tornado watch can remain in effect for several hours to several days.

tsunami A shoreward-bound series of large waves produced by an underwater disturbance such as an earthquake or a volcanic eruption.

tsunami warning system A system in which seismologists predict the creation of tsunamis by measuring underwater geological disturbances. When a tsunami is predicted, local authorities warn the public and give emergency instructions.

wind-safe room A shelter designed to provide protection from the high winds of hurricanes and tornadoes, and from flying debris.

For More Information

American Red Cross
National Headquarters
2025 E Street NW
Washington, DC 20006
(202) 303-4498
Disaster Assistance: (866) GET-INFO (866-438-4636)
Web site: http://www.redcross.org

Department of Homeland Security
National Disaster Medical System Section
500 C Street SW, Suite 713
Washington DC 20472
(800) 872-6367
Web site: http://ndms.dhhs.gov

Federal Alliance for Safe Homes
1427 E. Piedmont Drive, Suite 2
Tallahassee, FL 32308
(877) 221-7233
Web site: http://www.flash.org

Federal Emergency Management Agency
500 C Street SW
Washington, DC 20472
(202) 566-1600 or (800) 745-2520
Web site: http://www.fema.gov

See http://www.fema.gov/fima/tsfs02.shtm for information
  about building a tornado shelter.

National Flood Insurance Agency (NFIA)
(888) 379-9531
Web site: http://www.floodsmart.gov

National Hurricane Center
11691 SW 17th Street
Miami, FL 33165-2149
(305) 229-4470
Web site: http://www.nhc.noaa.gov

National Oceanic and Atmospheric Administration
14th Street & Constitution Avenue NW
Room 6217
Washington, DC 20230
(202) 482-6090
Web site: http://www.noaa.gov

National Weather Service
1325 E. West Highway
Silver Spring, MD 20910
(301) 713-0224
Web site: http://www.nws.noaa.gov

Pacific Tsunami Warning Center
Pacific Region Headquarters
737 Bishop Street, Number 2200
Honolulu, HI 96813
Web site: http://www.prh.noaa.gov/ptwc

U.S. Department of Health and Human Services
200 Independence Avenue SW
Washington, DC 20201
(877) 696-6775
Web site: http://www.hhs.gov/emergency/index.shtml

Web Sites

Due to the changing nature of Internet links, the Rosen
Publishing Group, Inc., has developed an online list of
Web sites related to the subject of this book. This site is
updated regularly. Please use this link to access the list:

http://www.rosenlinks.com/lep/toht

For Further Reading

Cantrell, Mark. *The Everything Weather Book: From Daily Forecasts to Blizzards, Hurricanes, and Tornadoes: All You Need to Know to Be Your Own Meteorologist* (Everything Series). Cincinnati, OH: Adams Media Corporation, 2002.

Dudley, Walter. *Tsunami Man: Learning About Killer Waves with Walter Dudley.* Honolulu, HI: University of Hawaii Press, 2002.

Hearn, Phillip D. *Hurricane Camille: Monster Storm of the Gulf Coast.* Jackson, MS: University Press of Mississippi, 2004.

Simon, Seymour. *Hurricanes.* New York, NY: HarperCollins, 2003.

Spigarelli, Jack A. *Crisis Preparedness Handbook: A Complete Guide to Home Storage and Physical Survival.* Alpine, UT: Cross-Current Publishing, 2002.

Verkaik, Jerrine, and Arjen Verkaik. *Under the Whirlwind: Everything You Need to Know About Tornadoes but Didn't Know Who to Ask.* London, England: Whirlwind Books, 2001.

Williams, Jack, and Bob Sheets. *Hurricane Watch: Forecasting the Deadliest Storm on Earth.* New York, NY: Vintage, 2001.

Bibliography

American Red Cross. "Disaster Service." Retrieved June 14, 2005 (http://www.redcross.org/services/disaster/0,1082,0_319_,00.html).

American Red Cross. "Hurricane." Retrieved September 14, 2004 (http://www.redcross.org/services/disaster/0,1082,0_587_,00.html).

American Red Cross. "Your Evacuation Plan." Retrieved September 15, 2004 (http://www.redcross.org/services/disaster/0,1082,0_6_,00.html).

Bonifield, Len. "For Older Homes, Check Your Tie-Downs." *St. Petersburg Times*, April 17, 2005. Retrieved June 12, 2005 (http://www.sptimes.com/2005/04/17/Homes/For_older_homes__chec.shtml).

FEMA. "Hazards: Hurricanes." Retrieved June 14, 2005 (http://www.fema.gov/hazards/hurricanes).

FEMA. "Hazards: Tornadoes." Retrieved June 14, 2005 (http://www.fema.gov/hazards/tornadoes).

FEMA. "Tsunami Backgrounder." Retrieved June 14, 2005 (http://www.fema.gov/hazards/tsunamis/tsunami.sht).

National Hurricane Center. "Hurricane Preparedness." Retrieved June 14, 2005 (http://www.floridadisaster.org/hurricane_aware/english/intro.shtml).

National Weather Service. "International Tsunami Information Center." Retrieved June 14, 2005 (http://www.prh.noaa.gov/itic).

National Weather Service. "Tornadoes: Nature's Most Violent Storms." Retrieved June 14, 2005 (http://www.crh.noaa.gov/lmk/tornado1/index.htm).

National Weather Service. "Tsunami Ready." Retrieved June 14, 2005 (http://wcatwc/arh.noaa.gov/tsunamiready/tready.htm).

Neuman, Peter G. "Anticipating Disasters." *Communications of the ACM*, March 2005, p. 128.

Pendick, Daniel. "Catching a Tsunami in the Act." Thirteen/WNET. Retrieved June 14, 2005 (http://www.thirteen.org/savageearth/tsunami/html/sidebar1.html).

Robinson, Andrew. *Earth Shock: Hurricanes, Volcanoes, Earthquakes, Tornadoes, and Other Forces of Nature.* New York, NY: W. W. Norton & Company, 2002.

Stark, Judy. "All About Plywood." *St. Petersburg Times*, April 17, 2005. Retrieved June 12, 2005 (http://www.sptimes.com/2005/04/17/Homes/All_about_plywood.shtml).

Tampa Bay Regional Council. "Planning, Patience, Go a Long Way." *St. Petersburg Times*, May 29, 2005. Retrieved June 12, 2005 (http://www.sptimes.com/ 2005/05/29/Hurricaneguide2005/Planning__patience_go.shtml).

Tuckwood, Jack, ed. *Mean Season: Florida's Hurricanes of 2004.* New York, NY: Longstreet Press, 2004.

Index

About the Author

April Isaacs is a writer and editor who grew up in Fort Wayne, Indiana, where tornado preparedness was a part of her early education. Her hometown has been in the path of several tornadoes over the past twenty years, including one that touched down in October 1992, hitting Fort Wayne International Airport. Ms. Isaacs has written several books for young adults. She lives in New York City.

Photo Credits

Cover (left) © Jim Reed/Corbis; cover (middle) courtesy of NASA ; cover (right), pp. 5, 12, 13, 19, 20, 28, 32, 33, 39, 42, 43, 46, 49, 51 © AP/Wide World Photos; p. 8 courtesy of the NOAA Public Library, NOAA Central Library, OAR/ERL National Severe Storms Laboratory (NSSL); p. 10 http://www.nws. noaa. gov; p. 17 by Tahara Anderson; p. 21 © Reuters/Corbis; p.24 © NASA/NOAA; p. 26 http://www.nhc. noaa.gov; p. 30 © Joe Skipper/Reuters/ Corbis; p. 37 FEMA Photo/Marl Wolfe, courtesy of FEMA;
p. 40 courtesy of the USGS, Earthquake Hazards Program; p. 50 http://www.sptimes.com/2005/webspecials 05/ hurricane-prep.

Designer: Tahara Anderson
Editor: Kathy Kuhtz Campbell